Would She Be Gone

A Censored City Novelette

MELANIE HARDING-SHAW

ISBN: 978-0-473-50176-1

This book is entirely a work of fiction. Any resemblances to real events, places, organisations, or persons is entirely coincidental.

The author acknowledges the excerpt quoted from 'Sonnet 66' by William Shakespeare. 'Sonnet 66' was first published in 1609.

Publisher:
https://www.melaniehardingshaw.com/

CENSORED CITY NOVELETTES

Would She Be Gone

Compact of Fire

Hell is Empty

CONTENTS

CHAPTER 1

"Are you sure you're up for this, Detective? Wires and comms won't work there. You won't be able to call for back-up if things go south."

Gini squared her shoulders and stood a little straighter. She knew the risks. This was the opportunity of a lifetime—undercover surveillance of a major crime syndicate. She might even get a medal out of it. It would make all the sacrifices worthwhile.

"Understood, Captain. You can count on me," she replied.

Captain Anders reached out to shake her hand. "We're behind you all the way, Detective. We need this win. You've got 20 minutes to prep. Detective Palmer will be your handler for the mission. Stay undercover as long as it takes. Dismissed."

Gini fought to keep her face to an appropriate expression as she left the room. She should have realised the operation was too good to be true. This was worth putting up with Palmer for, though.

Fifteen minutes later, she was pulling at the unfamiliar black wool turtleneck where it rubbed against her throat. She wondered how people wore this kind of thing every day. Her phone vibrated in her pocket and she checked the message.

Dad's not doing great. You coming tomorrow?

Her fingers stabbed at the screen as she typed a reply. The last thing she needed right now was a family drama.

I said I would. I'm working. Can't talk.

She'd barely hit send before the reply came.

You're always working. You better be there.

"Everything OK, Gin?" Palmer's voice called from behind her.

Gini spun around. "Of course, *Detective*."

"Oh. We're like that now?"

"Professional? Yeah."

Palmer shook his head. "Look, I said I'm sorry. Excuse me for thinking I had a right to care about you as a person. Is this going to be a problem?"

"No problem. Like I said—professional."

Palmer stared at her, and then sighed and looked away. "Fine. I'll take a different route to the meet and park on the corner of Jefferson and 7th. If you need me to follow you when you leave, take off your hat. Otherwise, we can debrief tomorrow in the park."

"Great," Gini said.

"It's not like I could have avoided talking to him, Gin. What was I supposed to do? Sit there in your lounge in a towel in silence?"

"Professional," Gini said again, and she turned and walked to her car.

She heard Palmer sigh again behind her, but he didn't call after her. What should he have done? Not open her damn door, especially to her brother. What gave him the right? She slammed her car door shut and pulled out of the carpark.

She was still fuming when she pulled into a park across from the bar. She sat gripping the steering wheel, breathing deeply. There was too much riding on this operation to let anything personal get in the way. She pulled on her black flat cap, used her mirror to apply a bright red lipstick and focused on who she needed to be. She steadied her hands and relaxed her face. By the time she was sauntering across the road, she doubted her squad would have recognised her.

The doorman inspected her inside the entrance to the bar.

"When to the sessions of sweet silent thought," Gini said, softly.

He looked her up and down. "All losses are restored and sorrows end. A good choice. You're new here. Who's your sponsor?"

Gini scrambled for an answer. No-one had mentioned a sponsor. She didn't even know where their intel had come from. It was that classified.

"Shakespeare," she said, raising her eyebrow as if she couldn't believe he'd asked the question.

"Sorry, I have to check. Can't be too careful. You'd be surprised how many newbies start naming people. Hand me your cell phone and you can head inside," the doorman said.

Gini passed her phone over and he placed it in a locker behind the desk.

"I just need to do a quick search before you go in," he said as he handed her a receipt for the phone.

She inspected the handheld device he was using as he meticulously scanned her. They had the latest tech. She wondered where they'd got it from. There was no way she could have snuck a recording device in.

"All clear. Enjoy your night."

She headed into the bar and ordered a glass of Pinot Noir before settling herself at a small table in a back corner away from the stage. She needed to avoid drawing attention to herself before she got the lay of the land. There were almost 50 people mingling or sitting at the other tables. She was surprised there were so many.

The polished wood of the tables gleamed in the flickering light from tealight candles and the thick red curtains by the stage looked like they would stand up to scrutiny in daylight. It wasn't exactly the dive she had pictured. The clientele was exactly as she had pictured them, though. The Gatsby hat had been the perfect choice to blend in. Hats and scarves abounded—anything they could use to hide their faces when they left.

Her glass was half empty when a man stepped up to the stage and began to speak.

"Welcome. Tonight's theme, as you know, is drawn from Shakespeare. In sonnet 66, he wrote:

And art made tongue-tied by authority,
And folly, doctor-like, controlling skill,
And simple truth miscalled simplicity,
And captive good attending captain ill:
Tired with all these, from these would I be gone,
Save that, to die, I leave my love alone.

I think those words speak down the ages to us here. Tonight, art will not be made tongue-tied by authority. There is no algorithm here deciding what you may hear or not. With your discretion, our poets will not be captive good. They will not be arrested for daring to speak to an audience that cares to listen. Because you do care. You care about freedom of speech and expression. You care about art and simple truth. Please, welcome our first poet!"

Gini took another sip of wine as applause sounded around her. She had to do something to cover her eye-roll response to that speech. Typical anarchists relying on the old 'freedom of speech' adage as if anyone was controlling what drivel these poets and authors produced. Just because they had a right to speak, didn't mean they had a right to inflict their words on the vulnerable. All the Librarian algorithm did was protect the vulnerable from mental health triggers—be they triggers of trauma or crime. It saved lives, unlike these so-called poets.

Gini got her anger back under control and paid attention to the stage again. A woman in her sixties was standing in front of the microphone adjusting the stand height. Her long grey hair was loose, partially screening her face from the watching crowd. She stood for a moment, composing herself, and then started to speak.

"I crashed a car at eighteen.
Quick, hide that Harry Potter and the willow scene,
and any other book where trauma is foreseen;
a literary vaccine.

Which is great, if the Librarian is free
from all subjective judgements and can see,
with unerring clarity,
every way in which those words I read have meaning to me.

Does your algorithm see inside my head?

Was it there the day I read my father Vonnegut on his deathbed?

Because the books you let him access could not distract him from his dread.

No. Instead,

You tore me from his dying exhalation.

Charged me with solicitation.

Ignored the comfort given by my narration.

And, in final insult, denied my right to be present at his cremation."

The woman's voice was cracking with emotion, the last word but a sobbed whisper. Gini reached up to scratch her cheek and frowned in surprise to find it wet. She swiped at the tear. It was just because the anniversary was so close, she thought. She didn't have anything in common with this woman. She had missed her mother's funeral for an entirely different reason. A valid reason. Unlike this lawbreaker.

A man who'd been leaning on the wall nearby approached her. "It can be pretty intense your first time," he said softly, offering her a tissue.

Gini forced herself to focus back on her mission and looked up at him, letting another tear leak out.

"Yeah. I hadn't really thought I'd be affected like that."

The first poet had left the stage and their place had been taken by the next.

"My name's Jonas. Mind if I join you?" the man asked.

"I'd like that. I'm Katherine. My friends call me Kat," Gini said with a smile.

She watched him surreptitiously as the next poet spoke. He had a hipster beard and a ridiculous flop of hair hanging down his forehead. Didn't these people even try to hide what they were? When the poet finished his performance, Jonas clicked his fingers in appreciation. Gini covered another eye-roll with her wine glass.

"I love the way his performance makes you forget the microphone is even there. He uses such mundane words, but it feels so intimate," Jonas said.

Gini had prepared for a conversation like this, drawing on distant memories of her mother from when she was a teenager.

"The language is what makes it intimate. As if he's talking to someone he's lived with forever. The rhythm is what keeps you hanging though."

"It reminds me a little of some of the rhythms Woolf used in her works. Do you think so?"

"I can't access them," Gini said with an ironic grin.

"Seriously? That's ridiculous!"

The people at the table next to them glared at Jonas for the loud outburst. The next poet was about to start.

"My mother was a writer who killed herself," Gini muttered with an awkward shrug.

The Captain had insisted she use her real history to ingratiate herself with these people. He'd said it would seem more authentic. Gini had almost told him to stuff his mission.

"I'm so sorry. I see why you reacted to Lauren's poem now," Jonas whispered back.

His face was set in that expression Gini hated. The one her workmates had worn for days after she missed the funeral, as if they could understand her loss. Damn the captain for being right.

"I lost my mother when I was 12. I don't think you ever really get over it," Jonas said.

Gini's eyes widened and Jonas gave her a sad smile of shared pain before returning his gaze to the stage. She let the emotions of the poet's words act as white noise for her own and ignored the niggle of guilt Jonas's words had set off inside her. It didn't matter that they had something in common. He was breaking the law just as much as anyone else here.

The MC came out to give a final speech at the end of the performance. Gini barely heard him as she tried to decide what the right play was with Jonas. If she came on too strong, she might give herself away.

When the applause faded, the audience stood and reached for their jackets.

"See you next time?" Jonas asked.

"For sure."

He tilted his head to the side and inspected her as if he was weighing how dangerous she might be. Then he reached in his pocket and grabbed a card.

"This is my number if you ever want to talk. I could get my hands on some Woolf for you, too. Or whatever else you were interested in."

Their fingers brushed as Gini took the card and she smiled. She couldn't believe it had been that easy. This could bust their case wide open.

"Thanks, Jonas. It was lovely to meet you," she said

Jonas leaned forward and kissed her on the cheek before waving goodbye.

She kept her hat on as she left the bar. Once she was safely in her car, she reached up to take it off. She was so lost in thought that she didn't notice her fingers lingering on the spot Jonas had kissed.

CHAPTER 2

The next day, Gini paused in her morning jog through the park to stretch under the shade of an oak tree. Palmer appeared a few minutes later.

"What took you so long? No-one stretches for this long mid-jog," Gini hissed at him.

"How'd it go? Got any leads?"

"I met a guy," Gini said.

"An important guy?"

Gini smirked at the hint of jealousy in his voice. This was going to be more fun than she'd thought.

"I don't know, yet. I've got to take it slow. I don't want to arouse suspicion."

"Shouldn't be a problem for you. Taking it slow has always been your strong suit."

Gini glared at him and turned her back to jog off.

"Wait! I'm sorry. That was unprofessional," Palmer said.

Gini paused and looked back at him. "Yes. It was."

"Do you need a ride to your dad's? You could have a few drinks with them. Relax a bit."

"For the last time. My family is none of your business. Back off!"

This time she didn't turn around when he called out after her.

She almost wished she'd taken him up on his offer when she arrived at her dad's that afternoon. He was sitting on the couch with her brother looking at pictures of her mum. Two empty bottles of wine nearby suggested they'd been there a while. They both looked up as she walked in and she felt the same old stab of grief and anger. Why did they have to wallow in memories of her? It was like picking at an infected scab.

"Hi, sweetheart," her dad said.

"You made it," her brother added.

"I said I would, didn't I?"

The two men on the couch exchanged a look and then returned to looking at the album.

"I can't stay long. Work's really busy," Gini said.

"Of course, it is," her brother said, his face twisting with sarcasm.

“That’s enough, George,” her dad said. He carefully enunciated each syllable, but Gini could still hear the drunken slur.

“So, what’s the deal? What kind of memorial are we doing?” Gini asked.

“Always in a hurry to get away,” George sniped.

“I said enough!”

Gini looked at her father in surprise. It wasn’t like him to get angry. She could see the tension in his face, as if he was bracing himself.

“Dad. You’re upset. We don’t have to do this today.”

George snorted back sarcastic laughter and their dad glared at him again.

“It’s the anniversary. We’re doing it today. Sit down!”

Gini sighed and sunk into a nearby armchair. It was the one her mother used to curl up in and write. Everything here was tainted with memories of her.

“You’ve avoided this long enough. We are remembering her properly today. Like we should have at the funeral.”

Gini burned with shame. Her fingers picked at a loose thread in the armrest.

“I couldn’t be there, Dad. I had to work. I didn’t have any choice.”

"You have a choice now. You don't even have to do anything. Just close your eyes and listen. Like she used to."

Gini winced. There was no getting out of this. She shouldn't have driven there. She could have been drunk. She'd done this to herself.

When she was a girl, she used to try and write stories and poems like her mother. Her mum had always said stories were made to be spoken. She would listen in careful silence with her eyes closed as Gini recited her latest attempt. Gini would hold her breath after she finished reciting and watch for the moment her mother's eyes would open and a brilliant smile would flash across her face.

"I don't need to close my eyes," she said through the aching pain in her throat.

"Please," her father added.

She sighed. "Fine."

She leaned back in the chair and shut her eyes. She heard her dad rustling in a bag nearby and then silence descended. Her breathing deepened as the quiet stretched to wrap around them like the blanket she used to nestle under when her mother read to her. Gini started as her father's soft voice sounded from nearby.

"There is a hole inside me, somewhere. A singularity that draws in all it touches. And everything that is me hovers on its edge, just past its event horizon—containing it even as it consumes me. I watch the light trickle out of the world like the vestiges of a draining ocean, leaving only memories flopping on the sand like drowning fish."

Gini was held captive by the voice and the words. She'd never heard her father speak like this before. As if he understood exactly how she felt every day, and felt that way himself too.

"And in the distance, I see figures moving. They carry buckets of water to pour upon the gasping fish, even though each bucket barely lasts a breath before it sinks into the grains of sand. I love those figures more than anything. I love each precious memory they protect. For a time, their love anchors me against the horizon's lure."

Gini felt her stomach drop down through the floor. This didn't sound like her dad. Her eyes flew open and she stared at him on the couch, holding a reader in his hands. A reader that wasn't his. For a moment, her professional-self wondered where he'd found a black-market reader and if Jonas was involved. Then panic set in. She was frozen in place.

"No, no, no. What have you done, Dad? Stop!" By the time she reached the last word, she was screaming.

He looked up from the reader. "You have a right to hear your mother's words, Virginia. No government should take that away from you. We got this reader for you. So you can make peace with her."

"I've got my work phone in my pocket, Dad! It monitors everything. The Librarian will have triggered an alarm already."

"But you wouldn't have listened if you knew what I was reading," her Dad replied, as if that explained anything.

"You would have kept pretending she was trying to hurt us. That she didn't care at all," George muttered.

She could see the heartbreak in his face. Gini opened her mouth to reply, but she was interrupted by the front door crashing open. She instinctively reached for the gun she wasn't wearing before she realised the people bursting into the room were police officers and raised her hands in the air.

"Edward Wright. You are under arrest for possession of an illegal reader and literary solicitation. You have the right to remain silent…"

Gini stared in shock as her frail father's wrists were twisted behind his back and handcuffed. The voice was relentless.

"George Wright. You are under arrest for aiding and abetting in literary solicitation…"

"No," Gini whispered. She closed her eyes and slumped back into her chair as the arrest carried on relentlessly.

"Detective Wright?" the voice asked, finally.

She looked up. She recognised the officer from her tour of cyber-crimes when she was first offered the undercover position.

"Jennings," she said in greeting.

"You're suspended until we can review all evidence and confirm you weren't involved. Hand over your badge and gun."

Gini stood up and pushed past him. "I'm on an undercover op. They're at the precinct already."

By the time she got outside, the patrol cars were already pulling away with the last of her family inside. She stood on the sidewalk staring after them. She was still standing there when Detective Jennings emerged from the house.

"What was he reading you anyway?"

"None of your damn business."

"Suit yourself. I'll hear when you give evidence at the trial anyway. The Captain said to tell you to book in for a psych eval while you're waiting to be cleared."

Gini peered closer at Jenning's expression. Her brain was slowly kicking back into gear.

"How did you get here so fast? And why aren't you arresting me? That's not protocol."

"Don't overthink it, Wright."

"Holy shit. This was a sting operation, wasn't it? Were my family the target or just collateral? Was anyone going to tell me?" Gini said.

"Go home, Wright. We'll call you when you're cleared."

Palmer was waiting by the door of her apartment when she got there.

"Did you know?" she asked.

"I knew there was another undercover operation going down. I didn't know they were arresting your family until they called me an hour ago. I swear."

Gini's hands were shaking so hard she fumbled the key in the lock. Palmer reached out to help.

"Back off! What are you even doing here? I'm suspended. Go *handle* someone else."

"Come on, Gin. Let me in. That's what friends do."

"I told you we're done."

"Yeah, well. You don't get to decide when I stop caring."

Gini glared at him, but Palmer already had his foot against the door to stop it closing. She threw the door open so hard it crashed into the wall and stalked to the kitchen to find the whiskey. Palmer was leaning on the doorframe watching her when she turned around with a full glass.

"You know, if you talk to me I can tell the Captain you don't need the psych eval," he said.

Gini swore under her breath. "Fine."

She shoved an empty glass at him and went back to the lounge. Palmer joined her on the couch a moment later and Gini shifted sideways until she was wedged into the corner.

"So, what did they get them for?" he asked.

"Possession and solicitation."

Palmer winced. "Damn. That's not good. Can't argue it's not premeditated with possession."

"Thanks. That's really reassuring. I feel so much better now. Are we done yet?" Gini slammed back the rest of her whiskey in one go.

"No. We're not done. What were they reading you?"

Gini stared at the dregs of amber liquid in her glass. She didn't want to talk to Palmer about it. She didn't want to talk to anyone about it. A psych eval would be worse though. Last time she'd barely scraped through.

"Something my mother wrote," she said.

"Oh, Gin. I'm sorry."

Gini got up to fetch the bottle of whiskey from the kitchen and poured herself another glass. She wished the lounge had enough room for more than a single sofa. When she got back, she avoided the couch and sat on the floor leaning against the wall. The last thing she needed was Palmer trying to hug her.

"Was it about… what she did?"

"Yeah. I think so. He didn't get all the way through it."

"Do you want to read the rest of it?"

"I can't," Gini snapped.

"That's not what I asked."

Gini took another sip of her drink. At least he wasn't hiding what we wanted to know. What the Captain needed to know. She would have seen through it if he had anyway.

"No. I don't want to read the rest of it. The whole point of the Librarian is to spare me that pain. What she wrote… it's exactly how I feel when I think about her. I don't want to read how that feeling turns into what she did. It could only end badly. I don't want to think about her at all. I just want to work."

Gini slammed back another whiskey and looked over at Palmer. His face looked pained. She poured herself another drink.

"What? No come back? No intrusive questions?" she asked when the silence had stretched too long.

"Gin, I think you need to talk to someone professional. Work can't be the thing that keeps you together. You can't just ignore that pain forever."

"Yes, I can. That's what the Librarian lets me do. That's why it's there."

"The Librarian is there to make space while you heal. That's not what you're doing." Palmer said.

"Really? Because my brother talked to people. He healed. And they still arrested him."

"Your brother had read it already. He told me about it when you were in the shower. We agreed it would be good for you to read when you were ready. He was trying to help you. He just went about it the wrong way."

The sounds of traffic in the background faded as a rushing filled Gini's ears. She dropped the heavy glass from numb fingers and watched as drops of liquid sprayed across the rug. The red wool made the amber whiskey look like old blood.

"Get out," she whispered.

"Gin, stop it. Stop pushing me away. I'm all you've got right now."

Gini launched herself to her feet and stood with shaking fists by her sides. What gave him the right to discuss her pain with her brother?

"You are going to leave. You are going to tell the Captain I am fit for work. Or I will tell him you encouraged my brother to commit a crime. You might not be fired, but there's no way they'll keep you on the taskforce if there's even a chance it's true. Get out. Now." Her voice was flat and her eyes were dead as she stared down at him.

Palmer's mouth dropped open. "You can't be serious. I didn't encourage him to do anything. I told him to share it when the Librarian gave you both access. When you'd healed. Calm down!"

Gini picked up her phone and started dialling.

"Stop! Fine. Have it your way. But I'm done trying to help you."

"I never wanted your help in the first place. The door's that way." Her hands weren't shaking anymore as she pointed. She was back in control.

Palmer shook his head and pushed past her outstretched arm as he left. "Goodbye, Detective."

"See you at work, Palmer."

CHAPTER 3

Whatever Palmer said to the Captain worked because she was reinstated two days later. She was sleeping on the couch when the call came. She knocked over an empty bottle of whiskey as she tried to grab for the phone and clutch her aching head at the same time.

"Detective Wright, you are cleared to continue your operation. Re-establish contact and proceed as planned," Palmer said.

"Copy that," Gini said and winced at the huskiness that came out in her voice.

"Are you drunk, Detective?" Palmer asked.

"Goodbye, Palmer."

Gini staggered to the bathroom and turned the shower on as hard as it would go. The needling points of water on her face drove her brain fog away. She checked the clock when she got out. Almost lunchtime. There was plenty of time to sober up before she reached out to Jonas tonight.

She went for a long run to clear her head and then fetched her new burner cell from the drawer she'd thrown it in the day before. She didn't trust Palmer anymore and she wasn't going to set up a meet on a phone he was monitoring. As far as he was concerned, she was taking it slow and she wouldn't have anything to report until the next poetry slam on Saturday.

Hi, Jonas. It's Kat. I've been thinking about your offer. I'd like to take you up on it, she texted.

She couldn't say anything more direct. A real buyer wouldn't risk the message being intercepted. She didn't have long to wait for an answer.

Sure. I'll be at the Vagabond tonight. Fancy a drink?

Gini frowned. She wasn't sure if they were just organising a clandestine meeting or if he was actually asking her out. It probably didn't matter one way or the other. She needed him to trust her. As far as she knew, the Vagabond was a legal music venue. There shouldn't be any risk of being caught in another sting.

See you at ten.

She abandoned sobering up around eight and had another couple of drinks before donning Kat's irritating tight clothes, hat and bright lipstick. She glanced at her police issued phone sitting on the table on her way out the door and left it where it was. She paused in the hallway. She wouldn't put it past Palmer to be surveilling her apartment to "keep her safe".

She headed up the stairs to the roof and made her way across two adjacent buildings and down a fire escape out of sight of any of the exits from her apartment. She had picked her home carefully. Palmer thought it was for the fire escape attached to her lounge window and the basement car park exit onto a back alley. She wondered which one he was watching. Probably the alley. That's the way she'd left after their first big argument. She always made sure her house-guests thought they knew her 'secret' ways out. There were six different buildings she could exit from along the rooftops. Seven if she didn't mind risking a one-story jump.

She was fashionably late to the meet, but Jonas didn't seem to mind. He was standing at a bar leaner with a couple of other men. They had obviously been drinking for a while because he threw his arms wide when he saw her and pulled her in to kiss both cheeks like they were in Europe or something. Gini was glad she'd had a couple herself already or she might have hit him. That's what she told herself anyway. Just like she told herself the smile breaking across her face when she saw him was just acting for the operation.

"Kat! You made it! What can I get you?"

She glanced at the table and saw three whiskey tumblers. "I'd love a whiskey. What are you drinking?"

"I like her already! It's a 20-year single malt from a small distillery a couple of hours away. They grow their own barley. I'm Pete by the way," the man to Jonas's left said, reaching out to shake her hand.

"And I'm Carlos. Don't listen to Pete. He wouldn't know his bourbon from his sherry casks," the other man said.

Pete punched Carlos' arm. Jonas laughed and steered her towards the bar and away from the sounds of his friend's bickering.

"Sorry about that. If you get them started on whiskey talk, it's all downhill from there," Jonas said.

His hand was resting lightly on the small of her back as they navigated the crowd and Gini smiled back at his too close face.

"No need to apologise. I'm usually more of a solitary drinker. It's nice to talk whiskey with someone," she said.

"Does that mean we have to go back and join them, or can I keep you all to myself?" Jonas leaned in close to speak softly in her ear. His words just audible past the sounds of the jazz band that had started playing on the stage.

Gini felt his warm breath on her face before he pulled back a little to watch her. His head was tilted to the side in question, and he didn't push any further as he waited for her response. Palmer's past insult sounded in Gini's head—taking it slow had always been her strong suit. Her eyes ran down the outline of Jonas's bicep through his shirt. Not just a poetry geek then. He clearly worked out. Gini laughed and wrapped an arm around him, pulling him closer and putting her other hand on his chest.

"You can keep all of me to yourself," she said.

The more they drank and danced, the more Gini felt her real personality melding into Kat's false one until she wasn't sure where one started and the other stopped. The only difference between them really was that Kat liked poetry and talked about her feelings.

Jonas already knew about her mother's death and it wasn't long before he'd extracted from her that the anniversary was only two days ago. In the darkness of a booth at the edge of the bar, she even let herself cry again in front of him, and was shocked to see his face traced with tears as well for their shared loss. No-one had ever cried with her before. She'd made sure they didn't get the chance.

Jonas shared memories of his childhood with his mother and her death—she'd found a lump one day and died three months later. He'd refused to go to the funeral, too angry at the world, and he'd always regretted it. They sat in silence for a minute when he finished talking, listening to the frenetic drum solo playing in the background.

"I told my family I had to work, but really I made sure I couldn't be there for her funeral. They've never forgiven me," Gini said. She'd never admitted that to anyone.

Jonas leaned in and gently kissed a salty tear on her cheek. She turned her face towards him without thinking and their lips met. His hand reached up to pull her in. Gini pushed away the cop-voice in her head telling her this was going to be trouble and the even louder voice telling her not to let anyone close. At that moment, she wasn't Gini. She wasn't anyone. She had no ID, no traceable phone. No-one knew where she was and she had no friends or family around to care anymore. She pushed her lips hard against his, relishing the pain of the pressure. She heard him groan in response.

"My place is three blocks away," his voice turned the statement into a question.

"What are we waiting for, then?" Gini replied. She felt his smile against her skin.

She woke the next morning on full alert before her memory caught up and she realised why she was sleeping in a strange bed. The smell of bacon drifted through the open door and she sat up, keeping the sheet pulled up to cover her chest.

She found her clothes crumpled on the floor and scooped them up so she could duck into the ensuite and get dressed. She stared at herself in the mirror—smudged lipstick and darkened eyes—and found a flannel to scrub at her face. How did people wear make-up all the time?

Jonas was putting plates on a small dining table when she left the bedroom. His hair was still damp from showering. Gini wondered how she'd slept through that. He looked up and smiled as he caught her movement.

"Morning. Come eat. If your head feels anything like mine, it will help," he said.

He leaned forward to kiss her as she joined him at the table. Gini hesitated a moment and then let him. In the sober light of morning, she was starting to realise this hadn't been her best idea. But the kiss brought back memories of the night before and she responded despite herself. Her hand knocked a fork to the ground as she reached for him, breaking the moment.

"Eggs are better hot," Jonas said, reluctantly.

"I've got plenty of time," Gini said.

She mentally kicked herself as the words came out and she felt herself smiling at him again. Maybe Palmer had been right and she did need professional help. Why couldn't she push this guy away?

Later that morning, they lay in bed together; Gini's head resting on Jonas's chest as he stroked her hair.

"I don't usually do this, you know," he said.

She looked up at him, a little surprised. She'd assumed one-night-stands were a poetry scene thing, a criminal thing.

"Me neither," she said.

"I could tell. I can see the effort it takes you to reach out," he said, softening the words with a smile in case she took it the wrong way.

Gini threw her pillow at his face. "Screw you."

She sat up, ready for the raging argument that her relationships always ended with. Instead, he just looked at her with that endlessly patient head-tilt. The one that didn't ask anything of her that she wasn't willing to give. Her scowl cracked into a rueful smile.

"Sorry. You're right, I guess."

He smiled and pulled her closer again, resting his chin on top of her head. "I'm away for work for the next couple of days, but I'd like to see you again. Are you going to the slam on Saturday?"

Gini made herself breathe calmly so she didn't give away her panic. Not a one-night-stand then. What was she getting herself into?

"Yeah. I'd like that."

Her mind was already whirling trying to figure out how to keep whatever their relationship was a secret from Palmer, who would be watching the entrance to the bar as her back-up. Jonas kissed her hair and then disentangled himself to get out of bed. She caught herself watching his naked form and looked away.

"I've got a reader here that you can have. You can access Woolf and whatever else you fancy on it. You can tell me what you think on Saturday," he said, as he detached a wall panel at the back of the closet to reach into a hidden compartment.

"Oh, wow. Are you sure?" Gini said, surprised at her sudden reluctance.

"Of course."

"This must have cost a fortune. Can I pay you something for it?"

Jonas laughed. "Don't worry about it. I get a bulk discount."

"Thank you," Gini said softly, clutching the reader to her chest with shaking hands.

Jonas sat next to her on the bed. "You look scared. Are you OK? You're way less likely to get caught reading this than turning up to a poetry slam. But if you're not comfortable, you don't have to take it."

Gini bit back a response about the exponential difference in prison time between attending a poetry session once compared to possession of an illegal reader. She scrambled for something to say that wasn't—I don't want to send you to jail for this though, you idiot.

"It's not that. It's just… I told you my mother was a writer, didn't I? I've never been able to read anything she's written. It's a little scary to hold her words in my hands."

Jonas pulled her into an embrace and held her tight. "You don't have to read anything you're not ready for. The decision is yours and no one else's."

Telling him about her mother's stories was only supposed to be a distraction, but it made her think. He was right. The decision was hers now.

"If you need anything, I'm here for you. Call me any time, OK?"

Gini shrugged and brushed away yet another tear in annoyance. When had she grown so soft?

"Promise me, Kat," he said.

"I promise," she whispered.

"Good. Now come have a shower."

Jonas made them sandwiches with the leftover bacon for lunch. When she finally opened the door to leave the apartment, he pulled her back to kiss her one more time.

"See you Saturday," he said.

His voice was firm, as if he knew she might try and back out once she left. She smiled and kissed him on the cheek, but as he closed the door behind her she spun and held it open.

"Jonas?"

"Yes."

"My real name is Gini. Virginia," she said.

His eyebrow raised a little and then he nodded.

"Nice to meet you, Gini. Most people give a false name at a slam," he said with a smile.

"Is Jonas your real name?" she asked.

"Yes."

"Would you tell me if it wasn't?" she asked.

He laughed. "Yes, Gini. I would. I was serious when I said you should call me if you need anything. You can trust me. You are now making me late for work though."

Gini smiled and kissed him through the gap in the door before making her way down the stairs and out into the daylight. It wasn't until she was two blocks away that she remembered how careless she was being. How had things gotten out of hand so quickly?

The smile drained off her face and she forced herself to refocus. She adjusted her route to take a more convoluted path back home and entered from a different building to the one she'd left from. She felt the corner of the illegal reader pushing against her side the whole way back.

CHAPTER 4

Gini's apartment felt cold and silent after the previous night. She sat on her small couch and stared at the reader in her hands. She needed to make a decision about Jonas, and she didn't think she could make it without reading the words he had returned to her through his gift of the reader. Plus, she needed to check that it did what he said it would. She'd be irresponsible not to, surely. Her father had already read plenty of the story aloud to her. Her restriction on reading her mother's works was really just a formality now anyway.

She powered up the screen and searched for Wright and the sentences she remembered from her father's reading. It was an excerpt from one of her mother's novels. The thoughts of a thinly-veiled self-modelled character.

There is a hole inside me, somewhere. A singularity that draws in all it touches… And in the distance, I see figures moving. They carry buckets of water to pour upon the gasping fish, even though each bucket barely lasts a breath before it sinks into the grains of sand. I love those figures more than anything. I love each precious memory they protect. For a time, their love anchors me against the horizon's lure.

Gini paused in her reading, waiting for the door to crash in again like last time. The silence still hung as heavy as ever. No-one was going to interrupt this time. She took a breath and continued reading.

There may come a day when I must set those figures free. Not because their arms and anchors are not strong enough, but because I cannot tolerate my black hole keeping them enslaved. Every moment spent trying to save what is already dead and worthless, instead of living in their own right.

She almost threw the screen across the room in rage. In her darkest hours, she had wondered if her mother didn't love her. If she had hated them all so much that she had taken her own life. This was so much worse. Her mother had thought she was saving her. That Gini's love and care for her was slavery. She had no right to make that choice. The chains of grief and guilt since her death were so much worse than the chains of love had ever been.

Gini sat and read. She read everything her mother had ever published. Three novels, two collections of short stories, and a book of poetry. As sleep deprivation took hold, she started arguing with the text; muttering to herself.

"No, you're wrong. Can't you see? Just give us another chance. Give me another chance. I can help you. You don't have to do it alone."

She reached the last stanza of the last poem. The last new words she would ever hear from her mother, delayed through years of censorship. She stared into the darkness, nauseous with hunger, eyes stinging with fatigue. There was nothing she could do. She had failed. Her mother was gone. Her knees curled up into her chest and her tears washed her into unconsciousness.

When she woke, her throbbing head was far worse than any hangover she'd ever had. She woke to the same thought she'd gone to sleep with: *you didn't have to do it alone*. She was damned if she was going to make the same mistakes her mother had. It was too late to help her mother, but it wasn't too late to help herself.

Her mother was right about one thing; she didn't have to spend the rest of her life enslaved. Jonas had given her something truly precious. She spent the next few days doing nothing but reading and rereading her mother's words until her phone ringing on Saturday afternoon yanked her back to reality.

"Detective? All set for another visit to the poetry underworld?" Palmer said when she answered.

"Of course."

"I'll be a block north of the bar. Same signal as last time if you need help."

"I don't need any help."

"You never think you do, Gin. Don't make me rebook that psych eval."

"Whatever."

She checked her burner phone and saw she'd missed five messages from Jonas. The final one read: *Gini? I'm worried about you. Please reply.*

I'm sorry. I disconnected while I was reading. I'll see you tonight.

Her phone buzzed barely a minute later.

Don't scare me like that! See you soon. I miss you.

She moved through her apartment like she was still asleep, staring into space as she showered and ate. She sat for five minutes on the edge of the bed with her right sock half on her foot, before shaking her head and yanking the fabric so hard it ripped a toenail. She cursed and went to the kitchen to pour herself a whiskey. She needed to get her head back in the game or Palmer was going to realise something was wrong.

When it was time to leave, she resisted the urge to take a back exit and public transport. Palmer would be watching from somewhere nearby for sure. Instead, she got into her police-issued unmarked vehicle and headed out to the bar.

Jonas was already sitting at a table when she arrived; waiting with two glasses of whiskey. There were no friends with him this time. He stood and kissed her cheek when she approached. Gini was too busy scanning the room to notice him pull away a little too quickly. Many of the crowd were the same as last time, but there were a few new faces. She had no way of knowing whether the Captain had sent another undercover officer in, or not.

She'd decided on the way there—whatever happened, she needed to make sure Palmer and the force didn't find out about Jonas. She needed to keep him safe. She owed him that much. She could figure the rest out later.

"How did your reading go?" Jonas asked.

Gini turned back to face him and took a sip of her drink to stall. Could she really trust him? She didn't have anyone else now and she was out of options.

"Life-changing," she said.

The simple word brought back all the emotions she was pushing down. Her face froze as she fought to keep control. Jonas reached out to squeeze her hand under the table.

"I hope in a good way," he said.

The first poet was about to start and Gini took the excuse to shift her chair around closer to Jonas to face the stage. She leaned close to his ear to whisper to him, letting her hair cover her face to mask the words from anyone nearby. She couldn't afford to waste any time. If Palmer or another undercover officer raised concerns, the Captain wouldn't hesitate to order a bust on the bar so the whole operation wasn't a failure.

"We need to talk. What you gave me changed everything. You changed everything. We can't be seen leaving here together."

When she looked over to gauge his response, she was surprised to see relief on his face. His broad smile, which she hadn't noticed was missing, had returned.

"How long have you known?" she said, as realisation dawned.

Her words were covered by the applause of the audience as the first poet finished. Jonas leaned towards her and gestured towards the stage as if he were commenting on the performance; his lips so close they brushed her ear.

"We suspected when you first showed up. The reader I gave you recorded your communications to Detective Palmer."

Gini glared at him. "How dare you spy on me!" she hissed.

"Is it so different from what you were going to do to me?" His voice was calm and reasonable.

"You used my mother's death to trap me."

"And you used your mother's death to lure me in when we first met."

"Is your mother even dead?" Gini said, struggling to keep her voice low. The people at the nearby tables were starting to look over at them, frowning.

"Yes," Jonas said. His voice was clipped, now, and his face had lost all expression. They sat staring at each other. No part of them touching anymore.

"I can't do this," Gini said.

She shoved her chair back and strode out of the bar; desperately hoping he remembered not to follow, even while a tiny voice inside her wished he would because it would mean he cared. She was a block away when Palmer's text came.

What happened? Why did you pull out? Is your cover compromised?

Shit, Gini thought. She needed to put him off. He couldn't find out. She needed time to figure out what she was going to do. She gritted her teeth and played to his protective bull-shit.

Someone started reading my mother's poetry aloud. Don't tell the Captain, please. It won't affect the operation. People cry in there all the time. They'll trust me more for it, Gini texted.

Are you OK? Do you want to talk about it? Palmer replied.

I'm fine. Are you going to tell the Captain?

I'll tell him it was part of a strategy. Playing the long game.

She paused with the key in the ignition as she typed a response. Then she rolled her eyes and bit the bullet. She needed him close or he would ruin everything. He needed to think they were friends.

Thanks, Cam.

I'm sorry about the other night, Gin. I've always got your back.

Gini didn't reply. She was damned if she was going to apologise to him. Thanking him was too much already.

Her burner phone buzzed with a message from Jonas on the way home. She didn't read it until she had a glass of whiskey in hand on the couch.

I'm sorry I hurt you. I'm not sorry I recorded you. You of all people should understand. I want to see you again. Ball's in your court.

Gini sat staring at the screen. She did understand. Damn him. It didn't make her any less angry. But she couldn't bear it if he left town thinking she was going to rat him out.

I get it. Your balls are safe with me.

Her mouth twitched when he replied with a laughing emoji and two kisses. Her fingers hovered over the screen.

I'm sorry, too, she wrote.

CHAPTER 5

Gini put up with Palmer's concerned texts for the rest of the weekend, ignoring them all. When her phone woke her up on Monday morning, she almost threw it across the room.

"What do you want, Palmer?" she said.

"Have you heard? I only just found out. I would have told you earlier if I knew. I promise," he said.

"What the hell are you talking about?" Gini said.

She was already pulling on her pants as she held the phone with her shoulder. She could hear in Palmer's breathless too-fast voice that something was seriously wrong.

"Your dad and your brother. They've signed a plea bargain with the DA. Sentencing is in an hour."

"But, their lawyer said they might get off with no conviction! Why the hell are they taking a plea bargain? I need to talk to them. Now!"

"It's too late, Gin. Their lawyer wasn't there when they signed. I'll meet you at the court."

Gini almost threw up from the anxiety spike when she saw the crowd gathered on the courtroom steps. It was a media circus. She'd never seen anything like it. There was no way this was going to end well for her family.

Palmer grabbed her shoulder from behind as she walked towards the building. She almost knocked him out.

"Calm down! It's just me. Wait up," he said.

Gini spun back towards the courthouse and kept walking.

"This isn't right. What's going on?" she demanded, gesturing to the cameras.

Palmer murmured to her so the journalists wouldn't hear. "I don't know. I swear. I have no idea what's going on."

Gini took the steps two at a time and paused to listen to a reporter speaking down the lens of a camera.

"The perpetrators of the widest literary solicitation ring ever prosecuted will be sentenced in court today. Fifteen offenders are expected to plead guilty to hundreds of offences between them. The case will be the first test of the sweeping legislative reforms to the Literary Safety Act passed on Friday after a surprise last-minute amendment was pushed through to make the new laws apply retrospectively to any outstanding prosecutions. In addition to harsher penalties, the changes will see new rights for police to access the biometric data recorded by readers. Critics are calling the law a breach of universal human rights. In a statement, the Minister for Literary Safety said the changes will save lives."

The reporter finished speaking and turned away from the camera. Gini tried to carry on into the building, but the woman had already seen the moment of unguarded despair on her face as she realised her family were stuck in the middle of a political shit-storm. She stepped in front of her, blocking her way.

"Are you related to the offenders? Do you have any comment?"

Palmer stepped in front of the camera that had swung towards them, pushing Gini into the building and covering her face with his jacket.

"We'll both be fired if your cover gets blown for coming here," he hissed in her ear.

Courthouse security stopped the cameras from following them, but the reporter ran to catch up. The woman pushed her card into Gini's hand, and then stumbled back with hands raised as Palmer shoved her away.

"I'm Deanna Myers. Here's my number in case you change your mind. Call me anytime," she said. She was watching Gini's face closely, looking for any sign she might have something to say.

"Back off!" Palmer said.

"Easy, mate. Let the lady decide for herself."

Gini tucked the card into her pocket as she watched the woman walk away. Palmer put an arm around her and steered her towards the courtroom.

"I'm sure it will be OK. They weren't part of the criminal ring. They were just small-fry customers," he said.

Gini pulled away from him. "It doesn't matter what they did. It only matters what the DA put down on the form and how much the judge wants to play with their new powers. I bet they didn't even know the law had changed before they signed."

They sat in the front row of the court. Gini's body hunched inwards, expecting the blow to come. Her spine pushed back hard against the wood of the benches as she braced herself against it. The point of pain was a lifeline of feeling as her mind went numb.

She didn't even notice the tears running freely down her cheeks when her father and brother entered the docks. They saw her there and tried to smile, but they must have realised something wasn't right. The flashes from court photographers filled the air like lightning as the pressure built. Palmer whispered to remind her to keep her face turned away from the cameras. He had to pull her to her feet when the judge entered.

The ritual of the court passed in a blur that Gini struggled to follow. She didn't wake from her daze until the collective gasp from the crowd behind her made her start. The first offender had been sentenced—25 years. Five times longer than any previous sentence, likely five times longer than the man had agreed with the DA. The judge was sending a message.

"He was the head of the operation. He won't do that to your family. It will be OK," Palmer whispered. He didn't sound like he believed it, though.

Her father and brother were the last to be sentenced. Her father was swaying as he stood, in shock from what had just occurred.

"Edward Wright, you plead guilty to one count each of solicitation and possession. Without people like you, these organisations would not be able to thrive. You purposefully and knowingly broke the laws of this country and, even worse, you showed a callous disregard for the mental health of your own daughter whom the laws were designed to protect. Yours is not a victimless crime. I sentence you to five years in prison."

The Court hadn't even taken a statement from her and they were using her pain to justify his imprisonment. Gini's eyes met her father's across the courtroom. She couldn't stand the guilt she saw there, but she wouldn't look away. He was so frail already. There was every chance he wouldn't make it through five years in jail.

"I love you," she mouthed silently to him and her brother, hoping they would see the words despite what seemed like a vast space between them.

Her brother winked in response, just like he used to when they had played a prank as kids and were about to get in big trouble.

"George Wright, you plead guilty to aiding and abetting your father. You had the power to stop this crime from ever occurring, and you chose not to. I sentence you to three years in prison."

Gini's head dropped then. Three years. Long enough to make travel to any other country impossible. Her brother had channelled his pain at their mother's passing into the international charities he volunteered for. He had lost that outlet forever.

Palmer pulled her to her feet again as the judge left, and she watched her family being herded out by guards like they were criminals.

"We need to wait until the press is gone. I shouldn't have let you come. I'm sorry," Palmer said.

His voice was shaking with nerves and he wouldn't look her in the eye. Gini resisted the urge to slap him. All he could think about was her stupid cover being blown. Who cared about that now? Her family's lives were ruined.

She felt her burner phone vibrate in her pocket and risked checking it while Palmer was distracted looking behind them at the photographers.

I saw what happened on the news. I'm here for you, the text from Jonas said.

Gini couldn't even bring herself to care anymore that he must have listened in to her conversation with Palmer this morning.

I'll come over later, she replied.

It was over an hour before Gini and Palmer could sneak out a side entrance from the court away from the watching media.

"I'll drive you home," Palmer said.

"I'd rather walk."

"It's safer if I drive you. No chance of a stray journalist recognising you."

"It's safer if I'm not seen with you. Piss off."

Palmer grabbed her shoulder and pulled her around to face him.

"Stop pulling that crap. Are you OK? Do you need to pull out of the operation? The Captain will understand."

"So my career can go up in flames, too?" Gini said, her voice flat and emotionless.

Palmer's expression softened. "Take a few days and then we'll talk. You're not thinking straight. There's no way you'll get out of a psych evaluation this time."

Gini blanched. She couldn't protect Jonas if she was taken off the operation.

"This is all I've got left," she muttered.

"We'll figure something out."

Gini shrugged and turned away. Palmer let her go. It wasn't long before she noticed a blue sedan trailing behind her; far enough back that Palmer thought she wouldn't notice. She kept her eyes forward and ignored him.

CHAPTER 6

Gini took the stairs to her apartment two at a time. She poured herself a drink as soon as she walked in the door and stared around the room vacantly trying to process what happened. Her eyes settled on the drawer where she'd put the illegal reader. She fetched it out and collapsed on the couch holding it in her hands. It was deceptively light; its rounded corners belying the stabbing pain it had caused her.

She couldn't face reading her mother's words again. Instead, she pulled up the text entry function and stared at the blinking cursor on the blank screen. She'd never tried to write anything before, and she didn't know where to start. She didn't want to rhyme like the slam poets and she didn't know how to make up characters like her mother had. But she needed to get the words out of herself; to bleed some of the pressure inside her away.

"Screw it," she said to the empty apartment. And she began to write.

This is my story. It is a true story, and it is a wake-up call to the world. If you choose to stay asleep after you read it, that's on you.

She stared at the words she had written, reading them over and over. She deleted them and started again.

When I was young, I would have nightmares of monsters. My mother would come hold me in the middle of the night, and pick up the story wherever my dream had left it. Her voice would fill the darkness with comfort. Her words would carry me to safety. Sometimes the monsters would be vanquished, but more often they would be redeemed. Someone would hold up a figurative mirror, and the monster would see the pain that they had caused. They would change. They would grow. That's what people do if they are given the chance.

Gini lost herself in the words she was writing. When she finally looked up from the screen, she had a thousand words or more. She sat steeping in despair. She needed Jonas.

She got changed, and turned her lights and television on so anyone watching her window would think she was still there. She turned her work phone off and slipped out to the rooftop. Palmer would assume she was drinking herself to sleep on her couch.

Hopefully, he knew better than to try and visit to comfort her. She pulled her hat down low to conceal her face as she walked towards Jonas's apartment.

When she reached the corner of his block, she paused to watch the people on the street. At least one kept glancing at his building. He could be one of Jonas's people or he could be another undercover officer. There was no way to know.

Gini looked around and saw a rubbish truck making its halting way down the street. She used it to screen her from view, before ducking down the alleyway to the building's fire escape. By the time the truck was pulling past the alley, she was already levering Jonas's window up to swing herself inside.

She froze at the sound of a soft click from nearby. Her body was hunched forwards and one foot was straddling each side of the window frame.

"Gini! I almost shot you!"

She looked over and saw Jonas putting a gun down on a side table. She never would have heard the bullet coming. She opened her mouth to reply, but no sound came out. Whatever had carried her this far was giving way and it was all she could do not to collapse to the floor.

Jonas crossed the space between them and pulled her into the room and his arms. They were still standing like that when the door crashed open and a man barrelled towards them. Gini tried to pull out of Jonas's arms, but he just held her tighter.

"It's OK, Pete. I knew she was coming. I just thought she'd knock first," he said.

The man stopped just short of them and looked a little sheepish. Gini recognised him as one of the whiskey-drinkers from the pub the other night.

"You were the one watching the apartment on the street. I wasn't sure who you were working for," she said to him.

He frowned and sighed. "I guess I need to work on my surveillance technique."

"I guess we both do. You guys spotted me as soon as I came into the bar," she said.

"Drink?" Jonas asked them, unwrapping his arms from around Gini.

"Doesn't he need to get back to his post?"

"Nah. There's two more outside. Count me in," Pete said, settling himself at the dining table.

Gini watched him warily, guessing he must be more than just a sentry. She trusted Jonas, but she didn't know anything about Pete. He pulled the chair out next to him and gestured for her to join him. She stayed standing. Jonas was returning from the kitchen with three glasses of whiskey. He put them down and came around the table to stand in front of her.

"You can trust us and we can help you, I think. If you want us to. There's never been a better time to push for change. People who've never protested before are already questioning what happened to your family."

"You want to use their story for your plans? Use my pain," she said in a flat voice.

Jonas reached out to stroke her arm. "Yes. But it's so we can stop what happened to them ever happening again."

He leaned forward and kissed her gently, and then joined Pete at the table. At least he was honest, Gini thought. She sat down between them.

"What's the plan?" she said.

"How do we know we can trust you? Jonas isn't exactly objective. I'm not putting years of our work into a cop's hands if there's any chance you could turn on us," Pete said. He was watching Jonas as he said it.

Gini looked down at her hands clenched into fists out of sight under the table. Now that she was starting to feel again, the anger was coming in waves every time she thought back to the sentencing.

It had been building since that first night she read her mother's words. It had been personal then, selfish even. Rage that a censorship algorithm had kept her enslaved to her grief and guilt for so long; the sense of betrayal when her fellow officers took her family away.

But sitting there at the table finally processing what had happened that morning, she realised she had been missing the point. She'd been looking for a simple place to lay the blame. It wasn't just the police or the rules programmed into the Librarian's AI. It was everything. The whole system.

It was the politicians who thought they could control people's thoughts; people who they were supposed to represent. It was the partisan judges that had lost sight of what was just. It was a population of people in denial about what they had lost; who didn't care because they didn't personally feel the pain, her pain. Thirteen other people's lives had been destroyed that morning, and many more would follow if nothing changed.

Gini raised her eyes to look at Pete. Nothing she could say was going to convince him she was trustworthy. There was only one thing that might. She took the illegal reader from her pocket and opened the file she had been writing. She pushed it into the middle of the table.

"Read that. I'm done with the police and this whole shitty system," she said.

She couldn't watch them read it. She didn't want to see their faces. She didn't want to see their pity. She hadn't held anything back in what she wrote—all her pain and anger laid bare in excruciating honesty. She may as well have cut her stomach open and poured her organs out onto the table.

She shoved her chair back and went to sit on the couch with her knees curled up to hide the room from view. She heard a chair leg drag on the floor as someone shifted around the table so they could both read. She felt the heat of her breath as it hit her jeans where her face was buried.

She forced herself to slow her breathing down—four counts in, hold for seven, eight counts out. The only practical technique she'd ever got from mandatory counselling; useful when you needed to focus to take a long-range shot. She wasn't going to lose it in front of them.

She heard murmuring voices, too low to make out, and then the door opening and closing. She still didn't look up. Jonas sat down next to her and held her tight against him, kissing her head.

"Pete's gone. He trusts you. I love you," Jonas said. Each sentence enunciated in the same matter-of-fact way.

Gini turned her face towards him, still curled tight around herself. "Because I'm broken and I hate the world?" she whispered.

That's why Palmer had loved her. She was a project to fix. Someone to make him feel needed. Not that he would have put it like that.

"Because you're strong. Because you're willing to learn and change your mind. Because you see a problem so big most people would give up and you say 'what's the plan?'. Because I can't be anything but exactly myself with you, even when I'm supposed to hide who I am, and I think you might be the same," Jonas said.

He drew back a little and waited for her response. Gini sat and tried to figure out if the person she'd pretended to be for him was actually her. Virginia Wright didn't open up to people. That wasn't who she was. But maybe that wasn't the point. Maybe the point was that she could have told him anything when she pretended to be the kind of person that shared her feelings, but she'd told him the truth. She hadn't even managed to keep her name a secret. He was right. Even when she was pretending to be Kat, she'd been exactly herself.

She wished she could make herself say something as heartfelt as he had in reply, but that was never going to happen. Instead, she unfurled her body and reached out to kiss him. She felt his mouth curl into a smile for a moment before he kissed her back. He got it. He got her.

The light from the streetlamps was shining through the window by the time they left the couch.

"So, what's the plan?" Gini asked for the second time.

"We have a piece of code. A virus, of sorts, created by the original programmer of the Librarian AI when she realised where things were heading. We've been working to find a way to spread it across the reader network."

"What does it do?"

"She called it 'Mary Sue'. It basically tells your reader that you're perfect in every way. No past trauma, no violent or depressive tendencies, no criminal or political 'radicalist' past to trigger censorship."

"Will that make any difference?"

"It's a start. People will begin to realise what they're missing. The censorship criteria have been expanding exponentially for the last couple of years without most people noticing. My organisation will release a lot of government information while the virus is active, so it doesn't get restricted. Stories of people like you. We can't force change. People have to want it. People have to fight for it. It will take time."

"So, how do you get the virus out there?" Gini asked.

"That's where you come in. The new laws give the police access to every reader in the country without a warrant to 'monitor biometric data that could reveal a crime'. Any computer in cyber-crimes will be able to access it. All we have to do is load the program and run a nationwide reader-search. The virus will do the rest."

Gini gritted her teeth in frustration. "I don't even have access at the moment. I'm on stress-leave until I pass a psych evaluation."

Jonas paused and seemed to choose his words carefully.

"Detective Palmer seems to have a… weakness… for you. Can we use that? We need to strike while people are still reeling from the court case. In a few days, they'll have moved on."

Gini forced herself to count her breathing again, fighting not to lose her temper.

"What exactly are you suggesting I do? Sleep with him? That's not going to make him break protocol to let me search the system."

"That's not what I meant! Do you really think I'd want that?" Jonas looked hurt.

Gini looked away, guilt replacing anger. "No. Sorry. Let me think."

She walked to the dining table and pushed at the reader she'd left there. The only reader in the country that contained the words she'd written. A plan started forming in her mind. She looked up at Jonas.

"What if I tell him your organisation is communicating through reader-to-reader coded messages? I could say the key-phrase changes every week with the slam themes. We can search the network for lines from the last slam. There should be plenty of readers with some of that poetry on them. They'll be chasing down leads for months."

Jonas was nodding. "That could work, but he might get suspicious at so many hits. Let's put a dummy phrase on this reader and say you stole it. I'll get my people to plant readers with matching phrases around town. See if we can't sneak some into the houses of those politicians that voted for the legislative reform. That should keep them busy accusing each other while we relocate. It won't be safe to stay here. Give me a couple of hours and we should be sorted."

"If I manage to get out. I'll disappear somewhere safe, too. You better not tell me where you're going, just in case," Gini said, not looking at him.

"Don't be stupid. I'll be waiting outside the station for you. All you have to do is get out of the building and into the car. It's a silver BMW. I'm not leaving you behind."

She glared at him, but she could see he wasn't going to back down. If he got himself caught, she would never forgive herself. Neither of them bothered discussing the fact that Palmer would probably arrest her on the spot when he realised what was happening, anyway.

It only took them a few minutes to cobble together a suitable phrase on her reader and plant the virus code behind it. Jonas kissed Gini long and hard before she climbed out the window to make her way back down the fire escape.

"Make it to that car, Gini. Don't make me come find you," he said.

Gini shrugged. "I'll do my best. Don't get caught with those readers."

The last thing she saw of the apartment was Jonas bent over the table copying the phrase onto every illegal reader he had stashed there while issuing urgent instructions to someone over his phone.

CHAPTER 7

Gini peeked over the edge of the roof when she made it back to her building. It was hard to tell what colour the cars parked by the back entrance were, but she could just make out a slight glow that could be the light of a cell phone coming from one of them.

She made her way down to her apartment and turned her work cell back on while she changed into the black cargo pants and leather jacket she usually wore at the precinct. A little of the tension left her body when she saw she'd only missed one message from Palmer. She had worried he might break her door down while she was out.

I'm here for you if you need me. Sent two hours ago.

She put the whiskey bottle and an empty glass on the table, and double checked the incriminating phone and reader were safely stashed in her pockets. Then she messaged him back.

Literally. Is that you outside my building? Creep.

That might have been a bit harsh, but she couldn't let him get suspicious. He needed to think nothing had changed. She poured herself a drink and waited. He was nothing if not predictable. She'd barely drunk half when he rapped on the door. She rubbed her eyes hard to make them look red and then opened it, whiskey still in hand.

"What do you want?" she said.

His eyes flicked from her face to the drink and back. "To help you, Gin. Stop pushing away the only friend you've got."

She stared at him and counted her breaths again as if she was trying to decide whether to trust him. Luring him in.

"I've got a lead. It's big," she said, finally.

"Great! How? When?"

"On Saturday, before… I needed to leave. I stole a reader from one of my marks."

"Gin! You didn't have a warrant! What the hell?"

"It's got a code-phrase on it we can use to trace the whole operation, but we need to search for it now before they change it. The warrant doesn't matter. We won't have to use the reader in court. We can just use it to identify the people to surveille," Gini said.

Palmer still looked dubious but he was calming down as he realised they could fudge it so it didn't undermine the whole operation.

"And you think you might be able to avoid the psych eval if you get a major breakthrough," he said, knowingly. "What exactly are we searching?"

"The reader network. They're using it to communicate. We can access the whole country, no warrant needed."

Palmer was nodding. "OK. That might work. We can try anyway. I'll take the reader in tonight and do the search."

"I'm not letting you take all the credit for this. Besides, there might be another layer of security I need to crack. I know these people better than you do. I need to be there. I need to stop them from luring innocent people to prison ever again," Gini said.

She thought she might have laid it on too thick, but Palmer was lapping it up. He reached out to hold her shoulder with an understanding expression on his face.

"You don't even have access to the building, Gin," Palmer said.

Gini stared at him until he looked away. "I'm not giving you the reader if you don't take me with you."

Palmer sighed. "Fine. Have it your way. You always do. We'll go after shift change. There are fewer people to recognise you on graveyard."

"I'll meet you outside in two hours," Gini said.

Then she shut the door on him. The less time she spent with him, the less chance he'd realise something was wrong.

She messaged Jonas while she waited. *Palmer agreed. Heading to the station at midnight.*

We'll be ready. I'll be at the side entrance on 3rd Street. Don't do anything stupid, he messaged back.

Palmer jumped in his seat when Gini knocked on his car window two hours later.

"One day you're going to sneak up on the wrong person and get shot," he said as she got in the car.

"Not if I shoot them first."

Palmer rolled his eyes and started the car.

"Are we going to talk about what happened this morning?" he said.

"Nothing to say. They were caught committing a crime. The judge sentenced them."

"You know I can see through that act, right?" Palmer said.

He reached out and squeezed her hand as he drove. Gini's body went stiff and she froze until he took his hand away.

"Was I really that bad?" he said, so softly she almost didn't hear him.

Gini looked out the window. She needed to shut this down before it messed up the whole plan.

"No. You're not that bad. You just always push. I need to work things through in my own time, not yours."

"Wow. That was… unexpectedly honest." He sounded impressed.

Gini kept her eyes trained on the city-scape passing by, the streetlights turning the structures sepia in the darkness like they were travelling through some old-time cop movie.

"Just because I don't talk about my feelings, doesn't mean I'm not dealing with them."

"Point taken."

They pulled into the precinct car park. Gini looked around for a silver BMW, but she was on the wrong side of the building anyway. Her mind started planning escape routes in case Jonas didn't show.

The desk sergeant looked up as they came in. "Detective Palmer. Can I help you? She's not supposed to be here."

Gini kept her face neutral and placed one hand on the reader in her pocket.

"I need her help sorting some paperwork before the captain looks over it tomorrow," Palmer said.

The sergeant grinned and shook his head. "Get behind again, Palmer? Alright. You better keep an eye on her though."

Gini opened her mouth to insult him and Palmer pulled her away down the corridor.

"Leave it, Gin."

"I'm not a damn baby."

"Stop acting like one then."

Gini glared at him and forced herself to keep walking. They were in. That was what mattered. The sooner she could leave this place forever, the better. Palmer sat down at the computer and logged in.

"We have to transfer the file across so the decryption key goes with it. Let me do it," Gini said.

She pulled up the search and synched the reader, careful to keep the adrenaline tremor in her hands under control. The transfer hung from the size of the hidden virus and Gini turned to Palmer to distract him, hoping he wouldn't notice.

"Thanks for doing this. I really appreciate it. I just need to know what happened to my family won't happen again. I need to shut it all down," she said. The truth was always more convincing.

He raised his eyebrows. "You're welcome. You really are changing. We can get through this," he said, reaching out to squeeze her hand again.

Gini resisted the urge to pull away and turned back to the computer as the notification popped up that the file had loaded. She set the search going and leaned back in the chair.

"Now we just wait. I'll start an email to the Captain explaining, and a list of the addresses as we get the hits," she said, pulling up another window.

The search had already found the first of Jonas's planted readers and marked it as a red dot on a map of the city. She copied the address across and started crafting a sufficiently convincing email for the Captain. She was so focused on writing that she didn't notice Palmer's silence. Another three addresses had been flagged before she thought to look over at him.

Panic stabbed through her as she saw he was engrossed in the reader; his eyes scanning across the screen obsessively. She hadn't locked it. There was only one thing on it that would have distracted him from the search—her writing.

"Gini, I'm so sorry. I never realised you felt like this," he said, as he looked up from the reader.

She stared at him in horror. It was one thing to bare her soul to Jonas and his criminal partner. She had never meant for it to be read by bloody Palmer. Partly because he was so insufferable, and partly because she didn't want his do-gooder self to go to jail when this whole thing blew up.

She did the only thing she could think of. She spun around in her chair and snapped out a punch that knocked him out cold before he'd even had a chance to register what was happening.

The search had broadened well beyond the city now, spreading the virus with it. She locked the screen and left it going. Hopefully, it would be enough. She couldn't stick around any longer to find out. She grabbed Palmer's gun and the reader, pausing to check he was breathing OK. She hoped the concussion wasn't too bad. With any luck, he'd have short-term memory loss and wouldn't be able to remember reading her story.

She messaged Jonas before she left the room. *Coming now. Search on track. Committed assault. You'd better be waiting.*

She forced herself to walk calmly down the hallways towards the side exit. She nodded to the desk sergeant having a coffee on his break as she passed the kitchen.

"Where's Palmer? Are you done with your paperwork?" he called out.

"Palmer's a pain in the arse. He can do it without me," she snapped.

The Sergeant smirked and went back to his coffee. It was exactly the sort of reaction he expected from her. She knew she only had a matter of minutes before he went to check on Palmer, though. She was supposed to be supervised.

She broke into a jog once she was out of sight. No time to mess around, now. If the station went into lock-down, she was screwed. She could see the exit up ahead. She was almost there.

"Wright? What are doing here?" Detective Jennings called from behind her.

He wasn't supposed to be on duty. She knew because they'd checked the duty roster before they came. He must have been called in. Someone had raised the alarm. She kept walking, ignoring him. She was four steps away from the door.

"Wright, freeze! I have my gun out. Don't make me shoot you."

She stopped where she was, one hand touching the door handle.

"Are you behind this hack? You trying to get back at us for your family?"

"I'm not trying to get back at anyone," she said.

"Take your hand out of your pocket. Slowly."

Gini turned to face him, opening the door a little as she did and wedging her heel against it to keep it in place. Her other hand was still in her pocket, feeling the smooth cold surface of Palmer's gun. She could shoot Jennings right now. He'd never see it coming. He'd probably shoot her, too. There wouldn't be any jail then. She could be free of it all. She'd done her bit.

She felt her phone vibrate against her leg. Jonas's reply. Jonas who was waiting outside and would probably be caught in whatever cross-fire she started. She wasn't her mother. She wasn't going to make the same mistakes. Her eyes caught a flicker of motion and she saw Palmer staggering down the hallway towards them. She watched him look from Jennings to her and back again.

"Who's there? Someone attacked me. I can't see properly," he called out.

"It's Detective Jennings. Hold your position, Palmer. I've apprehended Wright."

Palmer had almost reached him. Gini took her hand out of her pocket. She couldn't risk shooting him. She held both hands palm-outwards towards the two men. Then she blinked in surprise. Palmer was holding three fingers up just out of Jennings field of vision. Then two. Then one.

"I can't see you, Detective. You're all blurry. Where are you?" he said, stumbling into Jennings.

There wouldn't be another chance. Gini ripped the door open as the sound of Jennings' firearm discharging ricocheted around the hallway. That's what happens when you tackle someone pointing a gun at someone. Stupid Palmer and his stupid need to save her. He wasn't just going to get himself fired, he was going to get killed.

She was pulling the door shut behind her and running down the street before she felt the wetness running down her arm and realised it wasn't Palmer that had copped the bullet. Jennings had caught her in the shoulder. She swore.

For a panicked moment, she searched the empty street for a car. Then she heard the sound of an engine coming up behind her and spun around—a silver BMW. She yanked the door open and collapsed into the front seat as Jonas pulled away.

"You did it! The virus is still spreading. It's already gone far enough to make a difference. Our people are releasing the information. They won't be able to shut it down in time," Jonas said.

"That's nice," Gini said.

Her head was spinning and the darkness of the car seemed to be seeping into her brain. Jonas looked over at her in alarm.

"Gini? Shit! What happened?" Jonas slammed on the brakes.

"Got shot. Don't stop. I'll be fine."

Jonas grabbed a scarf from the back seat and wrapped it tight around her shoulder.

"No time. Drive," she said, pushing him away as the pain surged again.

He cursed and accelerated. They could hear sirens in the distance. There was no way to tell if their vehicle had been identified or not. Nothing to do but keep driving.

Gini pulled the reader out and opened the file of her writing. Then she fished a business card out of her pocket—Deanna Myers, the reporter from the trial. Before she could reconsider, she emailed it through to her. She'd never meant to share what she'd written, but they could be caught or killed at any moment. The words had convinced Palmer she was worth helping. Maybe they'd help tip the balance with the rest of the country, too.

Gini reached out and squeezed Jonas's hand where it rested on the gearshift.

Enjoy what you read? Reviews are always welcome. *Compact of Fire* is the next Censored City novelette.

You can subscribe to Melanie's newsletter at: www.MelanieHardingShaw.com

ABOUT THE AUTHOR

Melanie Harding-Shaw is a speculative fiction writer, policy geek, and mother-of-three from Wellington, New Zealand. Her short fiction has appeared in publications like Daily Science Fiction and The Arcanist, and she was a finalist for Best Short Story in the 2019 Sir Julius Vogel Awards.

You can find her at:
www.MelanieHardingShaw.com
Facebook @MelanieHardingShawWriter
Twitter @MelHardingShaw

www.ingramcontent.com/pod-product-compliance
Ingram Content Group UK Ltd.
Pitfield, Milton Keynes, MK11 3LW, UK
UKHW020415250726
13967UKWH00007B/2660

9 780473 501761